This Little Tiger book
belongs to:

_____

_____

_____

For Thomas and Maddie, with love ~ M C B
To Noah, Levi and Isaac ~ J C

LITTLE TIGER PRESS
An imprint of Magi Publications
1 The Coda Centre, 189 Munster Road, London SW6 6AW
www.littletigerpress.com

First published in Great Britain 2008
This edition published 2008

Text copyright © M Christina Butler 2008
Illustrations copyright © Jane Chapman 2008
M Christina Butler and Jane Chapman have asserted their rights to be identified as the
author and illustrator of this work under the Copyright, Designs and Patents Act, 1988

A CIP catalogue record for this book is available from the British Library

Printed in Singapore

2 4 6 8 10 9 7 5 3 1

The Dark, Dark Night

M Christina Butler   Jane Chapman

LITTLE TIGER PRESS
London

Frog was very excited. All winter he had been asleep under a stone, and now it was spring, he was on his way back to his pond.

On the way, he bumped into
Badger and Hedgehog.

Then he played leapfrog with
Rabbit and Dormouse.

Suddenly, he saw that it was getting dark, so he borrowed a lantern from Dormouse and off he went through the wood to the pond.

Woo-woo! the wind blew in the trees.

Squeak-squeak! went the lantern, as it swung from side to side.

And the dark was all around.

When Frog reached his home, he put the lantern down behind him and was just about to jump into the water, when he saw . . .

. . . a huge, black Pond Monster,
with enormous claws, coming
out of the reeds!

Frog grabbed the lantern and hopped as
fast as he could back through the wood.

"There's a huge monster in the pond!" he cried.
   "Are you sure?" laughed Hedgehog.
   Frog nodded, trembling.
   "All right," said Hedgehog, calmly. "We'll
have a look together."
   "And I'll come too," said Dormouse.

Off they went through the wood.
Woo-woo! the wind blew in the trees.
Squeak-squeak! went the lanterns.
"Wait for me!" cried Dormouse.
And the dark was all around.

Soon Hedgehog and Frog reached the pond.
"Now," said Hedgehog, "where's this
monster . . . ?"

"There it is!" cried Frog.

It was bigger than before, with enormous claws and terrible spikes down its back!

"Run! Run!" cried Hedgehog. "Pond Monster! Pond Monster!"

"What's all this?" chuckled Rabbit. "A monster? There's no such thing as monsters!"

"Come and see for yourself," said Hedgehog, shivering.

"All right," said Rabbit. "I will."

"I'll never swim in my pond again!" sniffed Frog as they set off through the wood.

Woo-woo! blew the wind in the trees.
Squeak-squeak! went the lanterns.
"Wait for me!" cried Dormouse.
And the dark was all around.

It wasn't long before they were back at the pond.
Rabbit, Hedgehog and Frog tiptoed to the water.
  There it was again, the big Pond Monster.
It was bigger than ever!
  It had enormous claws, terrible spikes down
its back, two big horns and wild waving arms!

"Run for your life!" yelled Rabbit, racing
back through the wood, with Hedgehog
and Frog close behind.

"What's going on?" asked Badger.
So they told him all about it.
"Come along," Badger said. "I'd
like to see this monster of yours."
And off they went once more.

Woo-woo! howled the wind.
Squeak-squeak! went the lanterns.
"Wait for me!" cried Dormouse.
And the dark was all around.

As they reached the pond, a huge gust of
wind came through the trees and blew out
all the lanterns!

"I can't see a monster," said Badger at last.
    "That's because it's too dark,"
whispered Frog.
    And there they all stood, waiting in
the moonlight for something to happen.

Just then, Dormouse caught up with the others, at last.

"Cooo-eeee!" she shouted, waving from the bank.

Badger, Rabbit, Hedgehog and Frog looked at Dormouse. And then they looked at the small, black shape waving from the reeds.

"Look at that!" said Hedgehog.
"That's not a Pond Monster," said Rabbit.
"That's Dormouse's shadow!" said Frog.
"Well, I never!" said Badger. "You were frightened of your shadows all the time!"

The four friends laughed and laughed and laughed. "Hurray!" cried Frog. "There's no monster after all!" And with a huge, happy

SPLASH!

he leaped into his lovely pond, at last.

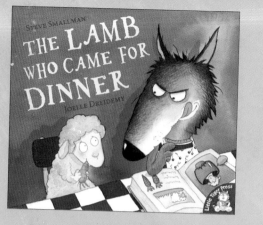

THE LAMB WHO CAME FOR DINNER

STEVE SMALLMAN
JOELLE DREIDEMY

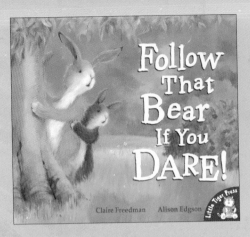

Follow That Bear If You DARE!

Claire Freedman   Alison Edgson

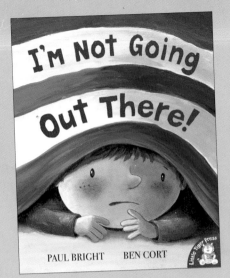

I'm Not Going Out There!

PAUL BRIGHT   BEN CORT

More EXCITING books from Little Tiger Press!

cock-a-doodle-hooooooooo!

Mick Manning   Brita Granström

AUGUSTUS AND HIS SMILE

CATHERINE RAYNER

Oodles of Noodles

Diana Hendry   illustrated by Sarah Massini

For information regarding any of the above titles or for our catalogue, please contact us:
Little Tiger Press, 1 The Coda Centre,
189 Munster Road, London SW6 6AW
Tel: 020 7385 6333 Fax: 020 7385 7333
E-mail: info@littletiger.co.uk www.littletigerpress.com